The Old Blue Pickup Truck

Candice F. Ransom

illustrated by **Jenny Mattheson**

Walker & Company
New York

First published in the United States of America in 2009 by Walker Publishing Company, Inc.
Visit Walker & Company's Web site at www.walkeryoungreaders.com

For information about permission to reproduce selections from this book, write to
Permissions, Walker & Company, 175 Fifth Avenue, New York, New York 10010

Library of Congress Cataloging-in-Publication Data
Ransom, Candice F.
The old blue pickup truck / written by Candice F. Ransom ; illustrated by Jenny Mattheson.
p.   cm.
Summary: As a girl and her father run errands in their old blue pickup, she discovers how many
different ways they can use their truck.
ISBN-13: 978-0-8027-9591-5 • ISBN-10: 0-8027-9591-9 (hardcover)
ISBN-13: 978-0-8027-9592-2 • ISBN-10: 0-8027-9592-7 (reinforced)
 [1. Fathers and daughters—Fiction. 2. Trucks—Fiction.] I. Mattheson, Jenny, ill. II. Title.
PZ7.R1743OI 2009   [E]—dc22   2008040316

Art created with oil on primed paper
Typeset in Shannon
Book design by Nicole Gastonguay

Printed in China by South China Printing Company, Dongguan City, Guangdong
(hardcover) 10 9 8 7 6 5 4 3 2
(reinforced) 10 9 8 7 6 5 4 3 2 1

All papers used by Walker & Company are natural, recyclable
products made from wood grown in well-managed forests.
The manufacturing processes conform to the environmental
regulations of the country of origin.

For Alex, who loves trucks! —C. F. R.

For my husband. —J. M.

Early one spring day, Daddy and I climbed into our old blue pickup truck and rattled down the road. We had lots to do.

First we stopped for bacon
sandwiches and hot chocolate.
The whipped cream in my
cocoa looked like a duck.
I blew it around my cup.

Daddy spread a bandanna on the seat
between us.
Old Blue was a restaurant.

Next we went to the plant nursery. Pots of flowers and vegetables grew in a glass house. Inside, it smelled like raindrops. Daddy chose tomato seedlings. The plant man gave me a rose.

Now our truck was a garden.

At the hardware store,
Daddy bought a new rake.
I filled a paper sack with
nails, one from each bin,
teeny tiny to great big.

Old Blue was a toolshed.

Daddy got boards at the lumberyard.

At the home store he bought a birdbath.

I found something just for me.

"Our truck is getting full," I said.

"Old Blue can handle it," said Daddy.

The next stop was the farm store.
Barrels filled with grain wore tin
scoops like party hats.

"That looks like cereal," I said.

"It's animal food," said Daddy.

"Are we getting an animal?" I
asked.

But Daddy was lifting sacks into our truck.

Now Old Blue was a feedstore.

We rode out of town and down a long, bumpy road.

We drove through a white gate and parked by a big red barn. Cows and goats nibbled clover. Rabbits napped in hutches, and a chicken chased a ladybug.

"Wait here," Daddy said.
Soon he came back with a
box. A damp pink snout poked
through one of the holes.
When he opened the top,
I saw it was a baby pig!

Daddy carefully set the box in the back.

Now our blue truck was a barnyard.

Daddy and I sang "Old MacDonald" as we rattled back down the road.

A drop of water went *splat!* on the windshield. Then there were more drops.

It was raining on all our things. Our whole day was getting wet!

"Uh-oh!" said Daddy. "The rake will rust. The feed will clump. The boards will warp. The plants will get overwatered."

"And the baby pig will be unhappy," I said.

"I wish I had brought a cover," said Daddy.

I had the perfect idea!

I gave Daddy my package from

the home store.

"A tablecloth!" he said.

We tied the plastic tablecloth
over the back end of Old Blue.

Old Blue splashed down the
road. By the time we got home,
the sun was shining.

Daddy and I planted and raked
and built a house for the baby pig.
But our busy day wasn't over.
   We polished and waxed our
trusty pickup truck until Old Blue
looked . . .

. . . as good as new!